NEIGHBORS

To Anna, the flutist, and
Tanya, the percussionist.
—K. D.

Library of Congress Cataloging-in-Publication Data available.

ISBN 978-1-4521-7775-5

Manufactured in China.

Design by Lydia Ortiz.
Typeset in Kasya Hand, a font created from the author's handlettering.
The illustrations in this book were rendered in ink.

10 9 8 7 6 5 4 3 2 1

Chronicle Books LLC
680 Second Street
San Francisco, California 94107

Chronicle Books—we see things differently.
Become part of our community at www.chroniclekids.com.

NEIGHBORS
BY KASYA DENISEVICH

chronicle books • san francisco

I know my new address
by heart:

3 Ponds Lane

Building 2

Apartment 12

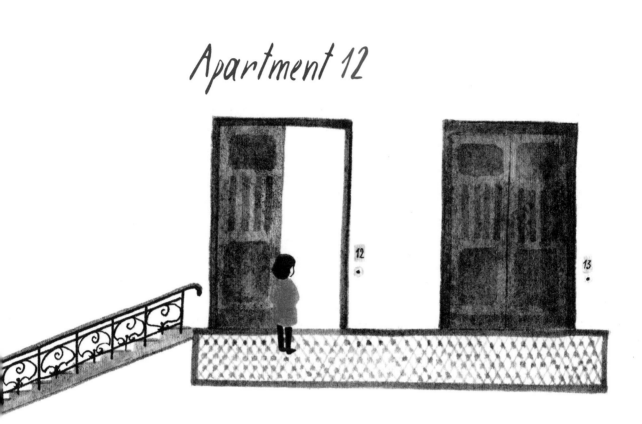

And I finally have a
room all to myself!

But if you stop to think about it...

My ceiling is
someone's floor,
and
my floor is
someone's ceiling.

If I could stretch
my hand through that
wall, I could actually
touch someone.
And that someone
is my new neighbor!

Neighbors are really all around me.
I wonder what they are doing right now.
Are they going to bed, just like me?

Do they look like me?
Or are they different in every way?

Are they at home?

Do they even exist?

Or maybe my building is my only neighbor.

What if there is nothing at all beyond the walls of my room?

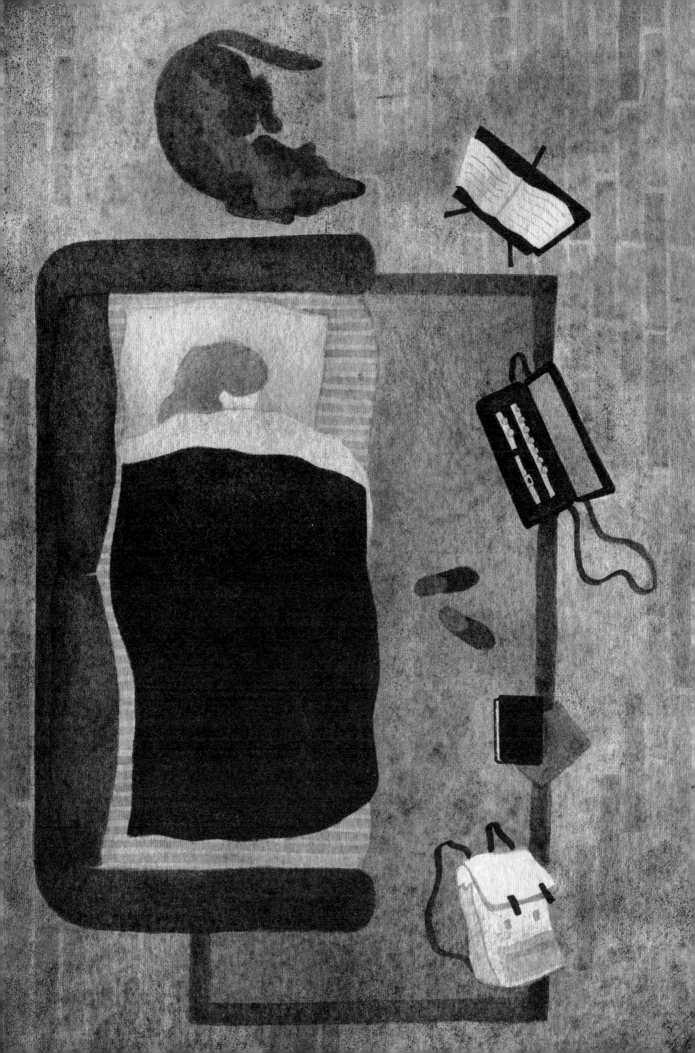

Well, TODAY is the day to find out.

Now what about my new
CLASSMATES?
I wonder what they're like.